Munschworks 4

The Fourth Munsch Treasury

Munschworks 4
The Fourth Munsch Treasury

stories by **Robert Munsch** and **Saoussan Askar**
illustrations by **Michael Martchenko**
and **Suzanne Duranceau**

annick press
toronto • new york • vancouver

Munschworks 4 © 2002 Annick Press Ltd.
Cover illustration by Michael Martchenko

Sixth printing, October 2011

50 Below Zero
        ©1986 Bob Munsch Enterprises Ltd. (text)
        ©1986 Michael Martchenko (art)
The Boy in the Drawer
        ©1986 Bob Munsch Enterprises Ltd. (text)
        ©1986 Michael Martchenko (art)
Moira's Birthday
        ©1987 Bob Munsch Enterprises Ltd. (text)
        ©1987 Michael Martchenko (art)
From Far Away
        ©1995 Bob Munsch Enterprises Ltd. (text)
        ©1995 Saoussan Askar (text)
        ©1995 Michael Martchenko (art)
Millicent and the Wind
        ©1984 Bob Munsch Enterprises Ltd. (text)
        ©1984 Suzanne Duranceau (art)

Annick Press Ltd.

We acknowledge the support of the Canada Council for the Arts, the Ontario Arts Council, and the Government of Canada through the Canada Book Fund (CBF) for our publishing activities.

Cataloging in Publication Data
Munsch, Robert N., 1945-
    Munschworks 4 : the fourth Munsch treasury / stories by Robert Munsch and Saoussan Askar ; illustrations by Michael Martchenko and Suzanne Duranceau.

ISBN 1-55037-766-3

    1. Children's stories, Canadian (English)
I. Askar, Saoussan II. Martchenko, Michael III. Duranceau, Suzanne IV. Title. V. Title: Munschworks four.

PS8576.U575M86 2002   jC813'.54   C2002-901345-3
PZ7

The art in this book was rendered in watercolor.
The text was typeset in Century Oldstyle and Adlib.

Distributed in Canada by: Published in the U.S.A. by Annick Press (U.S.) Ltd.
Firefly Books Ltd.   Distributed in the U.S.A. by:
66 Leek Crescent   Firefly Books (U.S.) Inc.
Richmond Hill, ON   P.O. Box 1338
L4B 1H1   Ellicott Station
                                             Buffalo, NY 14205

Printed and bound in China.

visit us at: **www.annickpress.com**
visit Robert Munsch at: **www.robertmunsch.com**

Contents

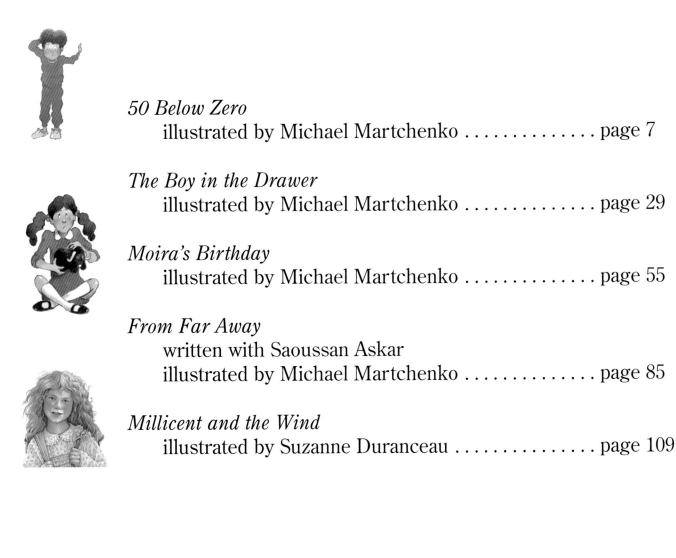

50 Below Zero
    illustrated by Michael Martchenko . . . . page 7

The Boy in the Drawer
    illustrated by Michael Martchenko . . . . page 29

Moira's Birthday
    illustrated by Michael Martchenko . . . . page 55

From Far Away
    written with Saoussan Askar
    illustrated by Michael Martchenko . . . . page 85

Millicent and the Wind
    illustrated by Suzanne Duranceau . . . . page 109

50 Below Zero

by Robert Munsch

illustrated by Michael Martchenko

In the middle of the night, Jason was asleep: ZZZZZ—ZZZZZ—ZZZZZ—ZZZZZ—ZZZZZ.

He woke up! He heard a sound. He said, "What's that? What's that? What's that!"

Jason opened the door to the kitchen ...

and there was his father, who walked in his sleep. He was sleeping on top of the refrigerator.

Jason yelled, "PAPA, WAKE UP!" His father jumped up, ran around the kitchen three times, and went back to bed.

Jason said, "This house is going crraaazy!" And he went back to bed.

Jason went to sleep: *zzzzz—zzzzz—zzzzz—zzzzz—zzzzz.*

He woke up! He heard a sound. He said, "What's that? What's that? What's that!"

He opened the door to the kitchen. No one was there.

He opened the door to the bathroom ...

and there was his father, sleeping in the bathtub.

Jason yelled, "PAPA, WAKE UP!" His father jumped up, ran around the bathroom three times, and went back to bed.

Jason said, "This house is going crraaazy!" But he was too tired to do anything about it, so he went back to bed.

Jason went to sleep: *zzzzz—zzzzz—zzzzz—zzzzz—zzzzz.*

He woke up! He heard a sound. He said, "What's that? What's that? What's that!"

He opened the door to the kitchen. No one was there. He opened the door to the bathroom. No one was there. He opened the door to the garage ...

and there was his father, sleeping on top of the car.

Jason yelled, "PAPA, WAKE UP!" His father jumped up, ran around the car three times, and went back to bed.

Jason said, "This house is going crraaazy!" But he was too tired to do anything about it, so he went back to bed.

Jason went to sleep: *zzzzz—zzzzz—zzzzz—zzzzz—zzzzz.*

He woke up! He heard a sound. He said, "What's that? What's that? What's that!"

He opened the door to the kitchen. No one was there. He opened the door to the bathroom. No one was there. He opened the door to the garage. No one was there. He opened the door to the living room. No one was there.

But the front door was open, and his father's footprints went out into the snow—and it was 50 below zero that night.

"Yikes," said Jason, "my father is outside in just his pajamas. He will freeze like an ice cube."

So Jason put on three warm snowsuits, three warm parkas, six warm mittens, six warm socks, and one pair of very warm boot sort of things called mukluks. Then he went out the front door and followed his father's footprints.

Jason walked and walked and walked and walked. Finally he found his father. His father was leaning against a tree.

Jason yelled, "PAPA, WAKE UP!"

His father did not move.

Jason yelled in the loudest possible voice, **"PAPA, WAKE UP!"**

His father still did not move.

Jason tried to pick up his father, but he was too heavy.

Jason ran home and got his sled. He pushed his father onto the sled and pulled him home. When they got to the back porch, Jason grabbed his father's big toe and pulled him up the stairs: *bump, bump, bump, bump.*

He pulled him across the kitchen floor: *scritch, scritch, scritch, scritch.* Then Jason put his father in the tub and turned on the warm water.

glug.

glug,

glug,

glug,

glug,

The tub filled up: glug,

Jason's father jumped up and ran around the bathroom three times and went back to bed.

Jason said, "This house is going crazy. I am going to do something." So he got a long rope and tied one end to his father's bed and one end to his father's big toe.

Jason went to sleep: *zzzzz—zzzzz—zzzzz—zzzzz—zzzzz.*

He woke up! He heard a sound. He said, "What's that? What's that? What's that!"

He opened the kitchen door ...

and there was his father, stuck in the middle of the floor.

"Good," said Jason, "that is the end of the sleepwalking. Now I can get to sleep."

In the middle of the night, Jason's mother was asleep: *zzzzz—zzzzz—zzzzz—zzzzz—zzzzz.*

She woke up! She heard a sound. She said, "What's that? What's that? What's that!"

She opened the door to the kitchen and ...

The Boy in the Drawer

by Robert Munsch
illustrated by Michael Martchenko

When Shelley went into her room, there
were socks on the floor, socks on the bed,
socks on the dresser, socks on the wall, and
socks everywhere.

"Yikes!" said Shelley. "What a mess."

And from out of the sock drawer some-
body yelled, "BE QUIET."

So Shelley crawled across the floor and
very carefully looked into the drawer. A small
boy was sitting there reading a book.

Shelley ran downstairs and said,
"Mommy, Mommy, there is a boy in my sock
drawer."

"Tell him to go home," said the mother.

"And there are socks all over my room."

"Clean them up," said the mother.

"But, but, but ..."

"Clean them up," said the mother.

So Shelley went back upstairs and looked
in the drawer. The boy was gone. She
cleaned up the whole room and went downstairs for lunch.

When Shelley went back upstairs, there was a large bump in the middle of the bed. She pulled back the covers and there was the boy, watering a tomato plant.

Shelley ran downstairs and said, "Mommy, Mommy, my bed is a mess."

"Clean it up," said the mother.

"But, but, but ..."

"Clean it up," said the mother.

When Shelley went back upstairs, the boy was gone. She cleaned up the whole mess by herself.

Shelley went downstairs and read a book. The room started to get dark. Shelley looked around and saw a big bump behind the drape. She very quietly crawled over to the drape and yanked it up.

There was the boy. He was painting the window black.

"Go away!" said Shelley. The boy grew five centimeters.

"Beat it," said Shelley. The boy grew five more centimeters.

Shelley took a paintbrush and painted the boy's ear black. He grew five more centimeters.

"Help!" yelled Shelley, and she ran off to find her mother and father.

They weren't in the basement and they weren't upstairs. They were in the kitchen. So was a lot of water. It was all coming out of the breadbox.

Shelley walked very quietly to the bread-box and yanked it open.

There was the boy. He was taking a bath. He said, "Please go away. You are bothering me."

Shelley had an idea. She turned the hot water all the way off, and she turned the cold water all the way on. When the cold water hit the boy, he jumped up, grew 50 centimeters, and sat in the middle of the kitchen table.

The father and mother both said,
"Shelley, tell your friend to go home."

So Shelley said, "Beat it."

The boy grew 10 centimeters.

Shelley decided to try something different. Very carefully, she walked over and patted the boy. Right away, he got a little smaller. Then her father went to the table and gave the boy a hug. He got very small.

Then her mother gave the boy a kiss, and he disappeared entirely.

"And who will clean up the kitchen?" said the mother.

"And who will clean up the kitchen?" said the father.

"And who will clean up the kitchen?" said Shelley.

And the mother gave Shelley a hug.

And the father gave Shelley a hug.

And she cleaned up the whole mess with no trouble at all.

Moira's Birthday

by Robert Munsch
illustrated by Michael Martchenko

One day Moira went to her mother and said, "For my birthday I want to invite grade 1, grade 2, grade 3, grade 4, grade 5, grade 6, aaaaand kindergarten."

Her mother said, "Are you crazy? That's too many kids!"

So Moira went to her father and said, "For my birthday I want to invite grade 1, grade 2, grade 3, grade 4, grade 5, grade 6, aaaaand kindergarten."

Her father said, "Are you crazy? That's too many kids. For your birthday you can invite six kids, just six: 1-2-3-4-5-6; and NNNNNO kindergarten!"

So Moira went to school and invited six kids, but a friend who had not been invited came up and said, "Oh, Moira, couldn't I please, PLEASE, PLEEEASE COME TO YOUR BIRTHDAY PARTY?"

Moira said, "Ummmmmm ... OK."

By the end of the day Moira had invited grade 1, grade 2, grade 3, grade 4, grade 5, grade 6, aaaaand kindergarten. But she didn't tell her mother and father. She was afraid they might get upset.

On the day of the party someone knocked at the door: rap, rap, rap, rap, rap, rap. Moira opened it up and saw six kids. Her father said, "That's it, six kids. Now we can start the party."

Moira said, "Well, let's wait just one minute."

So they waited one minute and something knocked on the door like this:

blam, blam, blam, blam.

The father and mother opened the door and they saw grade 1, grade 2, grade 3, grade 4, grade 5, grade 6, aaaaand kindergarten. The kids ran in right over the father and mother.

When the father and mother got up off the floor, they saw: kids in the basement, kids in the living room, kids in the kitchen, kids in the bedrooms, kids in the bathroom, and kids on the ROOF!

They said, "Moira, how are we going to feed all these kids?"

Moira said, "Don't worry, I know what to do."

She went to the telephone and called a place that made pizzas. She said, "To my house please send two hundred pizzas."

The lady at the restaurant yelled, "TWO HUNDRED PIZZAS! ARE YOU CRAZY? TWO HUNDRED PIZZAS IS TOO MANY PIZZAS."

"Well, that is what I want," said Moira.

"We'll send ten," said the lady. "Just ten, ten is all we can send right now." Then she hung up.

Then Moira called a bakery. She said, "To my house please send two hundred birthday cakes."

The man at the bakery yelled, "TWO HUNDRED BIRTHDAY CAKES! ARE YOU CRAZY? THAT IS TOO MANY BIRTHDAY CAKES."

"Well, that is what I want," said Moira.

"We'll send ten," said the man. "Just ten, ten is all we can send right now." Then he hung up.

So a great big truck came and poured just ten pizzas into Moira's front yard. Another truck came and poured just ten birthday cakes into Moira's front yard. The kids looked at that pile of stuff and they all yelled, "FOOD!"

They opened their mouths as wide as they could and ate up all the pizzas and birthday cakes in just five seconds. Then they all yelled, "MORE FOOD!"

"Uh-oh," said the mother. "We need lots more food or there's not going to be a party at all. Who can get us more food, fast?"

The two hundred kids yelled, "WE WILL!" and ran out the door.

Moira waited for one hour, two hours, and three hours.

"They're not coming back," said the mother.

"They're not coming back," said the father.

"Wait and see," said Moira.

Then something knocked at the door, like this:

blam, blam, blam, blam.

The mother and father opened it up and the two hundred kids ran in carrying all sorts of food. There was fried goat, rolled oats, burnt toast, and artichokes; old cheese, baked fleas, boiled bats, and beans. There was eggnog, pork sog, simmered soup, and hot dogs; jam jars, dinosaurs, chocolate bars, and stew.

The two hundred kids ate the food in just ten minutes. When they finished eating, everyone gave Moira their presents. Moira looked around and saw presents in the bedrooms, presents in the bathroom, and presents on the roof.

"Uh-oh," said Moira. "The whole house is full of presents. Even I can't use that many presents."

"And who," asked the father, "is going to clean up the mess?"

"I have an idea," said Moira, and she yelled, "Anybody who helps to clean up gets to take home a present."

The two hundred kids cleaned up the house in just five minutes. Then each kid took a present and went out the door.

"Whew," said the mother. "I'm glad that's over."

"Whew," said the father. "I'm glad that's over."

"Uh-oh," said Moira. "I think I hear a truck."

A great big dump truck came and poured one hundred and ninety pizzas into Moira's front yard. The driver said, "Here's the rest of your pizzas."

Then another dump truck came and poured one hundred and ninety birthday cakes into Moira's front yard. The driver said, "Here's the rest of your birthday cakes."

"How," said the father, "are we going to get rid of all this food?"

"That's easy," said Moira. "We'll just have to do it again tomorrow and have another birthday party! Let's invite grade 1, grade 2, grade 3, grade 4, grade 5, grade 6, aaaaaaand kindergarten."

From Far Away

by Robert Munsch
and Saoussan Askar
illustrated by Michael Martchenko

Dear Reading Buddy,

My teacher suggested that I write to you.
I will tell you about myself.
My name is Saoussan. I am seven years old and I am in grade two now.
I come from far away,

The place we used to live was very nice, but then a war started. Even where my sister and I slept, there were holes in the wall. Finally, one day, there was a big boom and part of our roof fell in. My father and mother said, "There is no food and we are getting shot at. We have to leave."

*My father left and was gone for
a long time. Then a letter came
with plane tickets to Canada.*

*I did not know anything about
Canada, but the next day I was
on a plane going there. As soon
as the plane moved, I got sick.
I stayed sick for the whole trip,
which was two days long.
I didn't like it. Nobody wanted
to sit near me.*

Once we got to Canada, my father took me to a school and left me there, after he showed me the girls' bathroom. He said, "Be good and listen to your teacher."

So I was good and I listened to my teacher, only I didn't know what she was saying because she did not know how to talk right. So I just sat and listened. Children were trying to talk to me, but I was not able to answer them because I didn't speak English.

When I wanted to go to the washroom, I didn't know how to say, "I want to go to the washroom." That's why I used to crawl to the door when the teacher turned her head and looked at the other side of the room. When someone opened the door, I crawled out and went to the washroom. When I came back from the washroom, I waited beside the door. When someone opened the door, I crawled back in and went to my desk.

Once, I crawled to the washroom and saw a Halloween skeleton, only I did not know what Halloween was. I thought the skeleton was evil. I thought that people were going to start shooting each other here. I screamed a very good scream:

Aaaa ahh hhhh hhh hh!

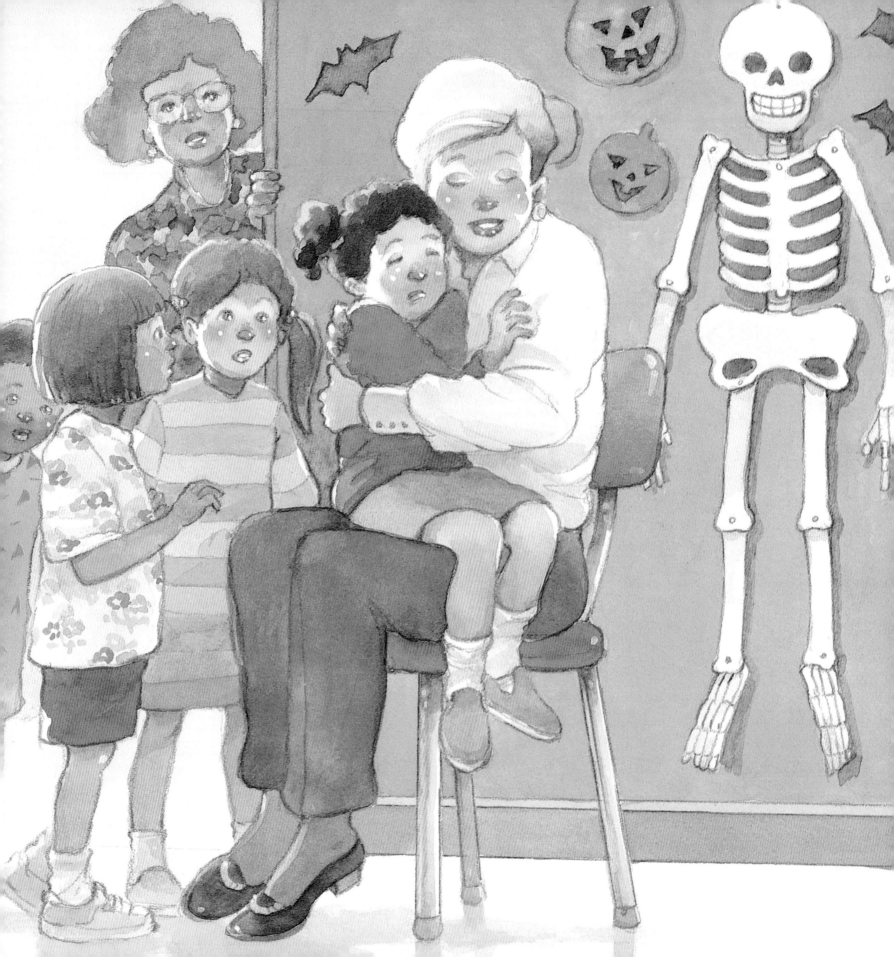

Everybody came running out of the rooms. They thought someone was being killed in the bathroom. My teacher opened the washroom door and tried to tell me that it was Halloween time and the skeleton was paper.

I didn't understand her and I didn't know what Halloween was. She jumped up and down and danced around to explain to me that Halloween is just fun, but I thought the skeleton made her crazy and I screamed louder:

Aaaa ahh hhhh hhh hh!

Then she hugged me to make me feel better. I felt as if my mother was hugging me. I jumped on her lap and pee went down my knees because I was scared to death. That happened so fast, and I felt guilty and ashamed of myself and I didn't know how to say, "I am sorry." But the big tear that went out of my eye said it for me.

Then I went and sat by the front door of the school till my father came and got me. I had decided that the whole school was crazy and I did not want to stay there.

When my father came, he told me about Halloween, and said that people here are not going to start shooting each other.

I had bad dreams about skeletons for a long time after that, but finally I began to talk, little by little. I learned enough English to make friends, and school started to be fun. Now I am in grade two/three and I am the best reader and speller in the class. I read and write a lot of stories. The teacher is now complaining that I never shut up.

This year when it was Halloween, I wore a mask and we had a party at school. Then I went with my sister trick-or-treating to the neighbors'. We got candy and nobody shot at us the whole time.

I decided that Canada is a nice place, and I changed my name from Saoussan to Susan, but my mother told me to change it back.

The kindergarten teacher moved from our school, but sometimes when I see her in the mall, I run to her and hug her and wish she was still my teacher. She was my first teacher in senior kindergarten and she helped me a lot.

But she still does not let me sit on her lap.

Goodbye,

SAOUSSAN

Millicent
and the
Wind

by Robert Munsch
illustrated by Suzanne Duranceau

One morning, when all the world was quiet, Millicent stood on her mountain-top and looked at the world. She saw trees and rocks and sunshine and clouds, but no other children. Far away in the valley was where the other children lived. It took three whole days just to walk there. Millicent had no friends.

n this morning someone whispered very softly, "Hey, Millicent."

Millicent looked all around, but all she saw were trees and rocks and sunshine and clouds.

Then someone whispered louder, "Hey, Millicent."

This time Millicent said, "There is nothing I see except trees and rocks and sunshine and clouds, and they cannot talk. Who are you?"

illicent," whispered the voice, "I am the wind."

"Oh, no," said Millicent, "the wind howls and roars and whistles and rustles. It doesn't talk."

Then the wind blew Millicent's dress around her legs, very softly touched her face and hair, and said, "I am the very wind of all the world. I blow when I wish and talk when I want to. The day is so quiet and the sunshine so yellow that I feel like talking right now."

ell," said Millicent, "I have no friends and lots of time. Can you play tag?"

"Certainly," said the wind.

So they played tag, running among the trees and the rocks and the sunshine.

"Come back tomorrow," said Millicent, and the wind did come back every day.

ut there came a time when Millicent was not there. She and her mother had gone down over the rocks and into the deep forest. They were walking all the way to the valley to buy the things they needed. So the wind could not play tag that day. It blew all over the world looking for Millicent, but Millicent was walking far at the bottom of a forest and the wind could not find her.

illicent and her mother walked for three days and finally came to the valley where people lived. When they walked through the valley, all the children came out of their houses and looked at Millicent. One boy with red hair said to Millicent, "Who are you and where do you come from?"

he said, "My name is Millicent. I live on the mountaintop. I have no friends except the wind." And the red-haired boy said, "The wind is nobody's friend," and all the children started to yell, "Millicent, Millicent, lives on a mountaintop! Go home, Millicent!"

123

hen a strange thing happened. A very large wind came and picked the red-haired boy right up into the sky and tumbled him around like a leaf until his clothes were all tatters and his hair was a mess.

All the children ran away. Millicent and her mother went to town and bought the things they needed, but Millicent was sorry that the children had run away.

 t took them three whole days to walk back to the mountain. When they got there, Millicent looked at the trees and the rocks and the clouds and the sunshine and wished that she had somebody to play with besides the wind.

ind," said Millicent, "you blow through the hair of every child everywhere in the world. Can you find me someone to play tag with?"

"Boy or girl?" said the wind.

"Get me a friend," said Millicent.

The wind turned into something huge and enormous that rumbled the rocks and bent the trees, and whistled off far away until Millicent could not hear it any more.

ut in a little while it came back, and it carried a boy.
The wind put him down.
Millicent looked at the boy.
The boy looked at Millicent.

"Let's play," said Millicent, and
they did.

The End

The Munsch for Kids series:

The Dark
Mud Puddle
The Paper Bag Princess
The Boy in the Drawer
Jonathan Cleaned Up, Then He Heard a Sound
Murmel Murmel Murmel
Millicent and the Wind
Mortimer
The Fire Station
Angela's Airplane
David's Father
Thomas' Snowsuit
50 Below Zero
I Have to Go!
Moira's Birthday
A Promise is a Promise
Pigs
Something Good
Show and Tell
Purple, Green and Yellow
Wait and See
Where is Gah-Ning?
From Far Away
Stephanie's Ponytail

Munschworks: The First Munsch Collection
Munschworks 2: The Second Munsch Treasury
Munschworks 3: The Third Munsch Treasury
The Munschworks Grand Treasury

Many Munsch titles are available in French and/or
Spanish. Please contact your favorite supplier.

How much Munsch have YOU read?

  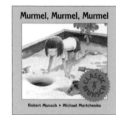  

Collections:

Drama: **Board Books:**

Have you read them all?